Thing

by

Chris Powling

Illustrated by Alan Marks

Published in 2006 in Great Britain by
Barrington Stoke Ltd
www.barringtonstoke.co.uk

ISBN-10: 1-84299-440-9
ISBN-13: 978-1-84299-440-5

Printed in Great Britain by Bell & Bain Ltd

A Note from the Author

Most of us are afraid of something – of ghosts, maybe. Or drowning. Or having a bad accident.

We're all afraid of *something* …

For me, one of the worst terrors in the world is thinking that someone is hunting me. I can't get away because the hunter knows me too well. And hates me because I'm trying to escape. In this story, *Thing* is a hunter like that. And I'd rather see a ghost, or drown, or have a bad accident any day of the week.

Thing is my own personal nightmare.

Contents

1   Alone   1

2   Found   4

3   Stuck Like Glue   11

4   Bad Joke   19

5   *Die*   28

6   Goodbye   36

7   Panic   41

8   Trapped   48

Chapter 1
Alone

There's a wind out in the garden.

There's rain in the air as well. I'm all alone

in my bedroom. The rest of the house is

dark. The only light I can see is here on my

desk. It's the glow from my computer as I

tap-tap-tap on the keys.

I should be feeling safe and cosy.

But I'm not.

I'm waiting for Thing. Just now Thing is creeping through the night. Sooner or later, Thing will slither under our gate and find a way to get into the house. By an open window, maybe? Or up a drain-pipe? It would take an army to protect me now.

That's why I'm writing this story. I just hope I get to the end of it before Thing arrives.

After that ...

Well, after that it'll all be over. You must make up your own mind what happened. Only these words I'm writing now will be left to tell you what went wrong between Thing and me.

That's if you've got the guts to read them.

Chapter 2
Found

Where did Thing come from?

No one was sure about that. Mum gave Thing to me one tea-time when I was just a kid. "Here you are, Robbie," she said with a smile. "You can have this."

"What is it?" Grandpa asked.

Mum gave a shrug. "Some sort of cuddly toy, I suppose. I found it up in the attic. The rest of the stuff up there was rubbish so I chucked it away. But this seemed like something worth saving."

"Do you think it's home-made?" Grandpa said.

"Looks like it," Mum nodded.

Thing was home-made all right. I saw that at once. It looked cut from an old T-shirt – or maybe from an old

dressing-gown. Whatever the cloth was, it could stand up by itself. The stitches were extra strong, too. They held Thing together like cord on the sail of a ship. Maybe an old seaman had made it on a trip round the world. It could have been his hobby when he wasn't on deck.

Great!

I really liked that idea. Thing wasn't your normal cuddly – not by a long shot. It had shiny black buttons for eyes. Its mouth was no more than a zig-zag across its face.

7

It had been made to last. This was a cuddly for one kid in a million.

No wonder I fell in love with it.

Thing was cool, OK?

I grabbed it from Mum's hands. Thing was *my* Thing right from the start – a good mate, a best ever toy and a big brother all rolled into one. From that moment on we were never apart. "Really!" Mum would say. "Sometimes I can't tell where that cuddly ends and you begin, Robbie!"

I couldn't tell, either. That's how it was for Thing and me. And that's how it would stay:

"Make up, make up,
Never ever break up ..."

Thing and I seemed to fit together like a key in a lock. Or a hand in a glove. Or a cork in a bottle. If you wanted to play with one of us then you had to play with the other. This was still true when I started school.

Chapter 3
Stuck Like Glue

I've moved on to Upper School now. So it feels like a hundred years since I first took Thing to Infant School. "No problem," the teacher told my mum. "Cuddlies are welcome here."

"Not a cuddly," I said.

"Well, a toy then ..." said the teacher.

"Not a toy!"

"A mascot, maybe?"

"Not a mascot!" I said. "It's *Thing*."

"Thing?"

"Thing!" I yelled and I stamped my foot.

"That's what Robbie calls it," Mum told her. "It is a bit ... well, *thing*-like you must admit."

The teacher smiled. "Robbie can call it what he likes, Mrs Price. I'd hate to spoil his first day at school. Welcome to Class 1, Robbie. And welcome to Class 1, Thing!"

Our teacher, Ms Scott, was lovely. So was everyone else at Infant School. They soon got used to Thing – the teachers, the helpers and the other kids in the class. I think Ms Scott was hoping I'd grow out of Thing in the end. So were Mum and Grandpa.

But I didn't.

"Make up, make up,

Never ever break up ..."

Break up?

Thing and me?

At the time it seemed that could never
happen. Thing sat next to me in class.
Thing went with me into Assembly. Thing
was always under my arm out in the
playground. No wonder his shiny black
button eyes looked happy. No wonder his

zig-zaggy mouth was always smiling. No wonder he sat up so tall.

Anyway, lots of the other kids took 'things' to school as well. Ms Scott would line them all up on a high shelf during lessons. There they sat – the dolls, the puppets and the teddy bears. Somehow, Thing was always smack in the middle.

Very stiff.

Very still.

Very silent.

So who ripped the dolls' dresses to
shreds when no one was looking? Who tied
the puppets up in a knot? Who yanked
clumps of fur from the teddy bears and bit
off their noses?

Ms Scott never found out.

It went on for term after term. As time
went by, more and more kids left their toys
at home. The risk of damage to their
cuddlies was too great. This made me very
proud.

Thing's shiny black eyes and zig-zaggy smile never shifted, you see – not even when Thing was left all alone on the shelf.

Chapter 4
Bad Joke

It wasn't like that in the Juniors.

Don't ask me why.

Somehow, cuddlies were out of order here – even a cuddly as weird-looking as Thing. At first, I took no notice of the whispers and the pointing fingers. Why should I let this upset me? But the teasing went from bad to worse. Even I got fed up with it in the end. So I started to leave Thing at home. "The classroom's too hectic," I told Mum and Grandpa. "I'm scared Thing will get messed about by the other kids. Or maybe even stolen."

"Fine," said Mum.

"Just as you like, Robbie," said Grandpa.

They winked at each other. I think they'd been expecting this to happen now I was older. I'd been expecting it myself to tell the truth. I mean, Thing was only a cuddly.

Or so I thought.

These days, Thing didn't look like a cuddly at all. Not even lying on my pillow. Those black, shiny eyes seemed a little *too* black and shiny. That zig-zaggy mouth zig-zagged a little *too* much. As for the stiff, crackly cloth which helped Thing stand up so tall ... wasn't it a bit *too* stiff and crackly?

21

"You'll soon get used to staying here, Thing," I told it. "Home's a lot better than school, you know."

But it wasn't better at all.

Not for Thing.

Thing wanted to be with me every moment of the day. I found this out all too soon. I'll never forget the moment when I opened my lunchbox in the hall. Thing was folded neatly inside – taking up every inch of space.

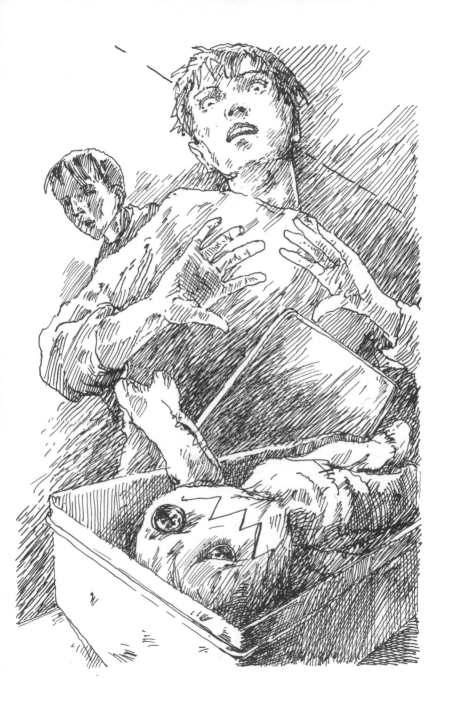

"Where's my lunch?" I yelped in alarm.

"What's *that*, Robbie?" asked my new mate, Greg.

"It's ... it's a joke," I stammered. "My Grandpa's always playing jokes on me."

"Doesn't look funny to me," Greg sniffed.

Nor me.

It wasn't funny at all – not with a mouth and eyes like that. And what about the stitches which held Thing together? Why did they suddenly look like *scars?*

Next time, Thing hid in my bag. After that, my football kit was the target. Then, worst of all, came my swimming stuff. As I unrolled my towel in the changing room, Thing flopped on the floor – all eyes and mouth and stitches.

Greg was amazed. "Another of your Grandpa's jokes?" he said. "He doesn't give up, does he!"

"Never!" I grinned.

Or I tried to grin. I didn't want to admit what was really behind these jokes. If you could call them jokes. They felt more like a test of strength to me.

And Thing was winning hands-down.

Chapter 5
Die

So I decided to fight back.

Against Thing?

I must have been mad. I see this now. At the time I thought I was being clever. Here are just some of the stunts I came up with to keep Thing out of my way:

I shut Thing in the fridge.

I locked Thing in the tool shed.

I buried Thing in the garden (twice).

I even nailed Thing to my bedroom floor as if by mistake. Nothing worked. Thing always found a way to escape. Before long, I was being followed to school almost every day. Suddenly, Thing would be there, grinning up at me.

"Make up, make up,

Never ever break up ..."

Break up?

Now that gave me an idea.

What was Thing made of, after all? Only cloth and cord and two shiny buttons, right? We weren't talking about something as hard as steel. So what if I fixed up a little run-in with Grandpa's lawn-mower? Or a fall into the front room fire? If that didn't do the job, we had an old loo at the back of the house. A flip of the lid, a splash in the pan, a tug at the chain and ...

BINGO!

No more Thing, OK?

Of course, I had to time it just right. Each try must look like an accident. If it didn't work, I'd have to wait a while or I'd give the game away. 'Slow and sure' was my motto. My aim was to get rid of Thing before I left Junior School.

Some hope.

I'll never forget the Leavers' Concert on the last day of term. By then, after attack number three, I was certain I'd flushed Thing out of my life. It was Greg who spotted something under my chair. "What's that, Robbie?" he asked.

"What's what?"

"That," said Greg, pointing.

To be honest, I was too shocked to say a word.

Was Thing really so cut to bits? Was it really so scorched all over? Did it really stink so much of the loo? Only one buttony eye had been left in place. The other hung loosely by a single thread. But nobody could mistake that zig-zaggy grin.

This had a nasty twist to it now.

Thing was angry.

Chapter 6
Goodbye

I know what you're thinking. Why didn't I tell Greg or Mum or Grandpa what was going on?

Pride, I suppose.

I didn't want to admit I needed help. Besides, I'd already got a new plan.

Somehow, by the time I got Thing back to the house, I knew just what I had to do. My new idea was brilliant. It was so simple, and so fool-proof, it couldn't possibly fail. Why hadn't I thought of it before?

Trust me, the parcel I put together that day was *secure*. On the outside it looked like a normal Jiffy bag. On the inside was Thing – stuffed into an old tin cashbox of Grandpa's. I'd sealed this with Super-glue. Then I'd lashed it together with wire. A rattle-snake couldn't have broken out of that lot. So what hope did a tatty, scorched cuddly have?

Now came the really clever part.

I sent the Jiffy bag to a small town deep in the outback of Australia. The address was *nearly* correct. Apart, from the person's name and street and house-number, that is. These I made up. I finished off with a stroke of genius. I gave the parcel to an uncle of mine to post for me in the USA. "My friend wants the post-mark for his collection," I said.

"No problem," my uncle nodded.

"Thanks!" I smiled.

Well, wouldn't you have been pleased with yourself? No one could track the parcel back to me now. It would be stuck forever on the other side of the world – on a shelf in some dusty Post Office.

Goodbye, Thing!

Chapter 7
Panic

The next four years were the happiest of my life. In all that time I didn't think about Thing. I was too busy making the most of Upper School. I'm a Prefect now. One day, I'll be Head Boy. That's what Greg says, anyway.

Yes, he's still my best mate. We hang out together whenever we can. Only yesterday, we were walking his dog Spike in the park behind my house. Every so often, we'd throw a stick for Spike to bring back to us. "Fetch, Spike! Fetch!" we'd call.

Which he did … if he was in the mood.

Greg thought this was funny. "One word from me," he said, "and Spike does as he likes!"

"He knows who's boss, all right!"

"Yeah, *he* is!" said Greg.

So Spike took us by surprise when he fetched a stick we hadn't even thrown. "Is it really a stick?" Greg asked.

"More like a strap," I said. "Or some kind of a ..."

... A noose.

That's what I'd nearly said.

But my voice had died away. This stick, or strap, or noose – what did it remind me of? I couldn't take my eyes off it. It had a much-travelled look – as if it had crept across half the world in terrible weather. The trip had dried it and thinned it down.

There it hung between Spike's teeth.

It was like a snake too limp to strike. At one end, still hanging by a single thread, was some sort of button, which glinted in the afternoon sun. "Just wait," the noose

seemed to be saying. "Just wait, Robbie, till I'm strong again..."

"Make up, make up

Never ever break up ..."

So I freaked.

I grabbed the thing from Spike's mouth. I threw it as hard as I could across the park. I didn't stop to see if Spike was chasing it. Or to see if Greg had clocked my panic. I was too busy racing all the way home as if I had every devil in Hell hot on my trail.

Chapter 8
Trapped

That's why I'm back in my bedroom. I've been typing these pages for hours now. My story will soon be over. And I don't mean with the words 'happily ever after', either. There's only one kind of ending here that I can think of.

There's still a wind outside.

It's raining, too.

So I won't even hear what's coming. Not a sound out in the garden. Not a thud here in the house. Not even the scrape of something sliding under my bedroom door.

But I'll feel it. I bet I'll feel it. Maybe I'll smell it, too – as Thing wraps itself tight round my neck. Is it too late to wake up Mum and Grandpa? Or give Greg a call on my mobile? Will they believe what I've written here or will they think I've gone raving mad? Will anyone ever believe me?

It must be worth a try. You should never give up hope, people say. Maybe all I need to save me is a little L

U

C

K

KK

KKK

KKKKKKKKKKKK

Barrington Stoke would like to thank all its readers for commenting on the manuscript before publication and in particular:

Susan Appleby

Mark Bain

Ryan Pattie

Become a Consultant!

Would you like to give us feedback on our titles before they are published? Contact us at the address below – we'd love to hear from you!

Email: info@barringtonstoke.co.uk
Website: www.barringtonstoke.co.uk

Also by the same author ...

Fight
by
Chris Powling

My Mate Could Take You ...

Matt's mate is a big, tough guy.

So that must make Matt hard too ...

Or does it?

You can order *Fight* directly from our website at
www.barringtonstoke.co.uk

More exciting NEW titles ...

Speed
by
Alison Prince

The Need For Speed

Deb loves to drive fast.

The faster, the better.

Until she goes too far, too fast ...

More exciting NEW titles ...

Alien
by
Tony Bradman

The World at War

The aliens are attacking!

Everyone must fight.

But just who is the enemy?

You can order *Alien* directly from our website at
www.barringtonstoke.co.uk

More exciting NEW titles ...

Stray
by
David Belbin

*Even in a gang,
she's on her own ...*

Stray's in with the wrong lot.

Can Kev save her?

Or will she drag him down?

You can order *Stray* directly from our website at
www.barringtonstoke.co.uk